SECOND BANANA

words by
BLAIR THORNBURGH

pictures by
KATE BERUBE

Abrams Books for Young Readers
New York

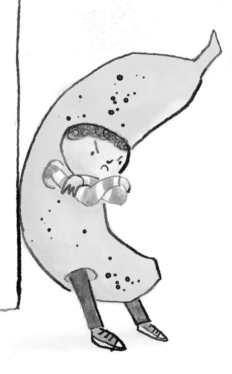

The illustrations in this book were created with ink, Flashe paint, acrylic paint, and colored pencils on cold press watercolor paper.

Cataloging-in-Publication Data has been applied for and may be obtained from the Library of Congress.

ISBN 978-1-4197-4234-7

Printed and bound in China
10 9 8 7 6 5 4 3 2 1

Abrams Books for Young Readers are available at special discounts when purchased in quantity for premiums and promotions as well as fundraising or educational use. Special editions can also be created to specification. For details, contact specialsales@abramsbooks.com or the address below.

Abrams® is a registered trademark of Harry N. Abrams, Inc.

ABRAMS The Art of Books
195 Broadway, New York, NY 10007
abramsbooks.com

To Bo
—B. T.

For Nan, Carrina, Megan, Liz, and Martha,
who took loving care of my daughter
so I could make this book
—K. B.

Food Is Fun
Healthy Eating
Good Nutrition
Pageant

CASTING
TODAY!!

Every year, the fifteen kids in Mrs. Millet's class put on the famous Food Is Fun Healthy Eating Good Nutrition Pageant.

Every kid plays a food.
Every kid gets a line.

It is a big deal.

But this year, we have sixteen kids.
That is a big deal, too.

Mrs. Millet has a plan.
"Don't worry, class. I need every last one of you.
Your families will love it—you'll see."

We all get our roles:

Bread

Rice

Fish

Chicken

Sugar

Butter

Cheese   Broccoli   Carrot

Pea   Eggplant   Pepper

Blueberry   Pineapple   Banana

And guess who ends up having to share?

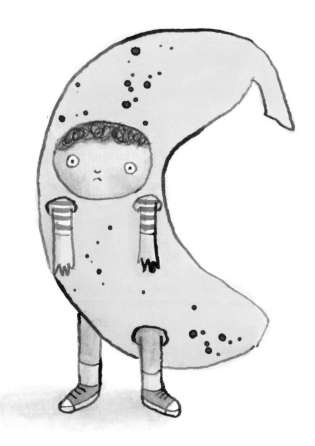

Second Banana

I do not want to be Second Banana.

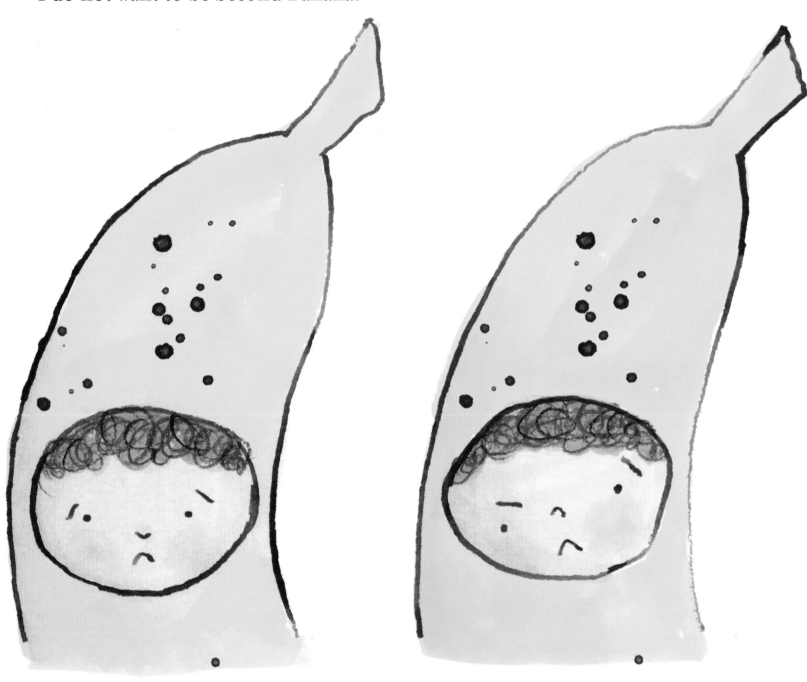

I want to be the *only* banana.   Second Banana gets only half a line.

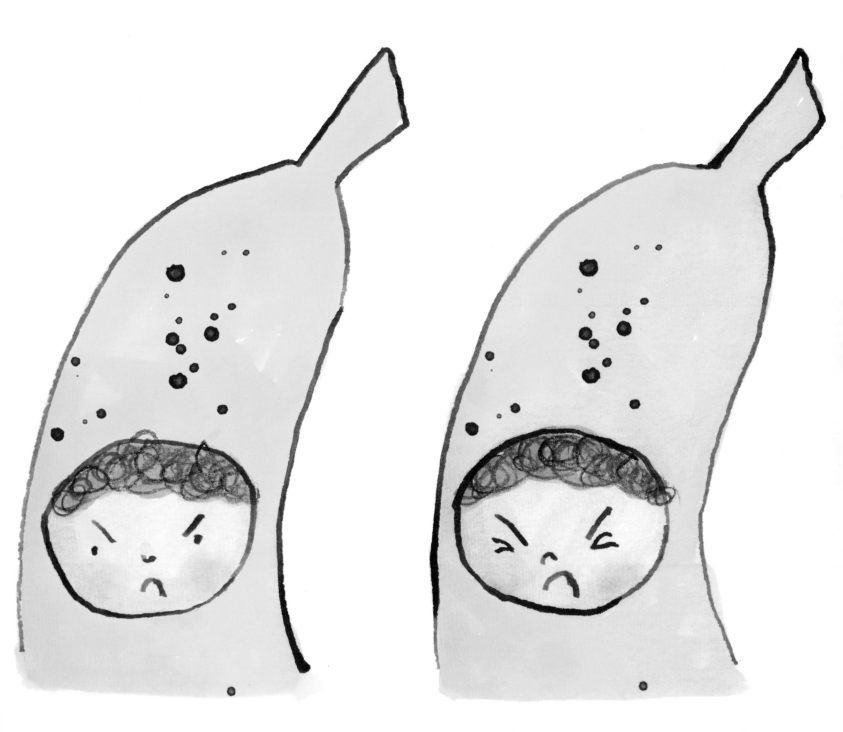

Second Banana barely fits onstage.

Second Banana is just not special.

Mrs. Millet doesn't understand.

"Don't you worry. You'll be like peas in a pod!"

Two peas? That makes sense.
But we don't have two pea costumes.
We only have two *banana* costumes.

And I do not want to be Second Banana.

My family doesn't help.
"This part is *ripe* for acting," says Mom.
"It's such an a-*peel*-ing role," says Dad.
"Just don't slip and fall," says my sister.

Not. Funny.

"But I do not *want* to be Second Banana!" I tell them.
"I want to be the *only* banana!"

I feel rotten.

All month long, we rehearse the
Food Is Fun Healthy Eating Good Nutrition Pageant.

Bread and Rice give you pep and power.

Broccoli and Cheese build bones and teeth.

Sugar and Butter are used sparingly.

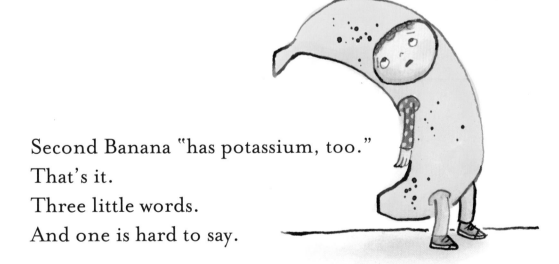

Second Banana "has potassium, too."
That's it.
Three little words.
And one is hard to say.

We rehearse over

and over

and over

and over.

Until . . .

"Get excited, class!" says Mrs. Millet.
"Just two days to go! The best pageant yet!"

I am not excited.
I still feel rotten.

And . . .

. . . it looks like
First Banana does, too.

Even with the better part,
with more lines,
and more to do,
and more time onstage.

"I didn't want to be Second Banana," I whisper. "I wanted to be the only banana."

First Banana whispers back, "I don't want to be onstage at all."

At *all*?
But every kid plays a food. Every kid gets a line.
It is a *big deal*!

And I don't want First Banana to feel rotten.

"This part is *ripe* for acting!" I tell her.

"It's such an a-*peel*-ing role!"

"I won't let you slip and fall!"

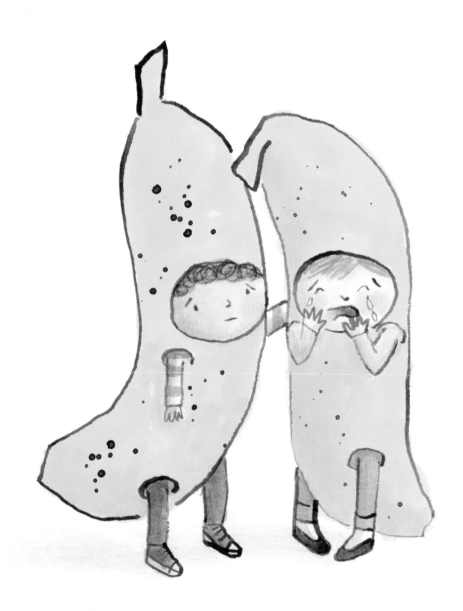

First Banana still does not look sure.

But the show is tomorrow. So I find Mrs. Millet. Because I have a plan.

"Let's change things up. A special finale.
Our families will love it—you'll see."

On the night of the show, the curtains flutter. The lights fill the stage.
The crowd murmurs in their seats.

The Food Is Fun Healthy Eating Good Nutrition Pageant is about to begin.

Bread forgets her lines.
Cheese misses his cue.

Sugar and Butter are used sparingly.

But the crowd
laughs and claps.
They eat it up.

And then
it's time
for dessert.

We come out together, one on each side.

"Our show is now over—"

"—remember it's great . . .

"—but before the end—"

when you *split* with a friend!"